W9-CFN-101

a  b

 **c**

An Alphabet
Book of
Cats and
Dogs

 **d**

by Sheila Moxley

Megan Tingley Books

 Little, Brown and Company
Boston New York London

First Edition

ISBN 0-316-59240-4

LCCN 00-035671

10 9 8 7 6 5 4 3 2 1

TWP

Printed in Singapore

The illustrations for this book were created using photographic prints and acrylic paints.
The text was set in Catchup, and the display type is Futura Heavy.

For Rick
and Cricklewood

Aa

Arnold is an amazing aviator.

Bb
Beatrice balances beautifully on her ball.

Cc

Carlos wears a checkered cap in his convertible.

Dd

Deborah delivers doughnuts door-to-door.

Ee

Edward enjoys eating eggs.

Ff

Freddie fishes for flounder.

Gg
Ginger grows geraniums

Hh

Henrietta has her hat on.

Ii

I van is gliding on ice.

Jj
Joe jumps and jives to his
jazz saxophone.

Kk

Ll

Louise longs for letters from her love.

Mm

Ming masters a magic trick.

Nn

Oo

Oswald often orders orange juice.

Pp

Patrick paints pet portraits
with his paw.

Qq

Quentin curls up quietly on his quilt.

Rr

Renée races around in her
rocket ship.

Ss

Sam sails the seas on sunny days.

Tt

Tabitha taps her tambourine with perfect timing.

Uu

Ursula stays underneath her umbrella.

Vv

Victoria buys a violin on
vacation in Venice.

Ww

Wendy wears weird wigs on
Wednesdays.

Xx

Xavier is an excellent xylophone player.

Yy

Yolanda yearns for a yellow yo-yo.

Zz

Zack and Zelda like to nap in their zebra-striped blanket . . .
ZzZzZzZzZzZzZzZzZzZz.

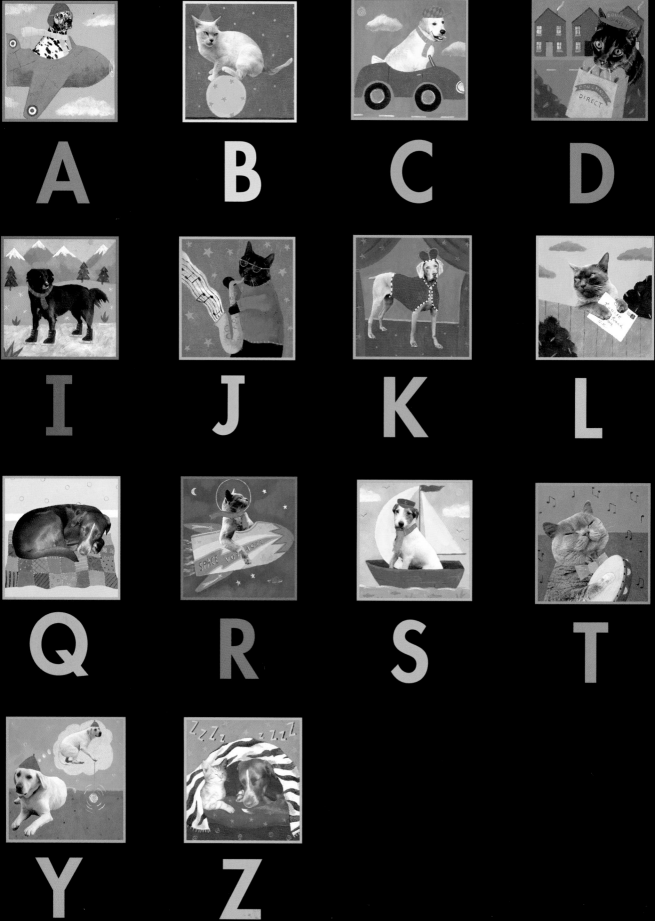

A B C D

I J K L

Q R S T

Y Z

E   F   G   H

M   N   O   P

U   V   W   X

A note about the artwork in this book:

No computers were used in the creation of the art — although this could change as soon as I become computer-literate! For now, there's no substitute for some old-fashioned painting and a bit of cutting and sticking with a scalpel and some sticky-tape. Most important, I had a plentiful supply of photos so I'd like to thank all the cats and dogs who cooperated and allowed me to take their pictures. In fact, I'd even like to thank the ones who didn't cooperate and hid behind the sofa, or zoomed up the nearest tree as soon as I got my camera out!

—S. M.